3/03

SkySisters

For the SkyDwellers
and
To All my Sisters
especially my big sister, and Allie and Alexei — J.B.W.

For Alex, Eric and Lee.
Thank you Vicki, Dad and Sharon — B.D.

❄

The Anishinawbe Ojibway words in the story are
Nishiime, which means "younger sister" and is pronounced *Ni-shee-may;*
Nimise, which means "older sister" and is pronounced *Ni-mi-say;* and
Nokomis, which means "Grandmother" and is pronounced *No-ko-mis.*

Text © 2000 Jan Bourdeau Waboose
Illustrations © 2000 Brian Deines

Kids Can Press acknowledges the support of the Ontario Arts Council, the Canada Council for the Arts
and the Government of Canada, through the BPIDP, for our publishing activity.

Published in Canada by
Kids Can Press Ltd.
29 Birch Avenue
Toronto, ON M4V 1E2

Published in the U.S. by
Kids Can Press Ltd.
2250 Military Road
Tonawanda, NY 14150

www.kidscanpress.com

The artwork in this book was rendered in oil on canvas. Text is set in ITC Berkeley Oldstyle.

Edited by Debbie Rogosin
Designed by Karen Powers
Printed and bound in Hong Kong by Book Art Inc., Toronto

This book is smyth sewn casebound.

CM 00 0 9 8 7 6 5 4 3 2

Canadian Cataloguing in Publication Data

Waboose, Jan Bourdeau
Skysisters

ISBN 1-55074-697-9

I. Deines, Brian. II. Title.

PS8553.A26S59 2000   jC813'.54   C00-930334-0
PZ7.W32Sk 2000

Kids Can Press is a Nelvana company

SkySisters

Written by Jan Bourdeau Waboose

Illustrated by Brian Deines

Kids Can Press

"Hurry and finish your hot chocolate, Alex," my big sister calls.
She pulls on her blue parka and scoops her gloves off the floor.
"Come on, slowpoke, or they'll be gone by the time we get there."

I gulp the last drop of chocolate and wipe my mouth on my sleeve.

Mother smiles. "Dress warm," she says.

Sister holds open my new green parka. It is my favorite color. I slip my arms in, then lace up my boots.

"Allie, I'm not slow. See, I'm ready."

Mother looks out the window. "Yes, the SkySpirits will come tonight," she says.

"Let's go!" I shout, and I race to the door.

Mother calls after me. "Alex, remember to listen to Allie."

"Yes, Alex, I'm older." Allie grins.

"Not by much," I say.

Mother raises a finger to her lips and quietly says, "Shh, remember the words of Grandmother, our Nokomis. *Wisdom comes on silent wings.*" She smiles and waves, then closes the door.

The night air is cold and tickles my nose. I watch my breath form clouds that greet the open sky. My big sister and I stand beneath a million stars. Nothing stirs. Silence is all around us.

Everything is frozen, except for me in my parka and my sister in hers. I think of our journey ahead and my heart beats faster. I am filled with excitement and I wonder how quiet I can be.

My sister's soft words break my thoughts. "Keep warm, Nishiime." She calls me this to remind me that I am the little sister. She reaches over, flips up my hood and tucks my pink scarf around my face. Then snuggles behind her own warm scarf.

"We might have a long wait tonight," she says as she creates a trail ahead of me through the blanket of snow.

"How long?" I call out.

She does not answer my question but turns to me and says, "Shh, Nishiime, whisper when you speak." She raises a purple-gloved finger to her lips.

"Okay, Nimise." I form the words but make no sound.

Our boots leave big holes in the snow as we head in the direction of Coyote Hill. Sister leads the way. I follow in her footprints. Her stride is bigger than mine, so it's not easy to keep up.

I remember the stories Mother told us about midnight on Coyote Hill. When she and Aunty were girls, Mother was the leader. Aunty was younger and had to follow like I do. I wonder if Aunty ever wanted to lead.

I eat snow from my mitten as I trail behind.

Up ahead, Nimise is waving her arms for me to hurry.

"I'm coming!" I blurt the words into the night. My voice flies through the air. Then I remember the words of our Nokomis. I can't see my sister's face, but I know she is frowning.

We stop by a gathering of trees. I watch Nimise pluck a glistening icicle from a branch and put it in her mouth. I do the same. Quiet surrounds us, except for the sound of my sister sucking on her ice sword.

"You're noisy," I whisper.

She sticks out her tongue and moves on. I ignore her and look up to see Grandmother Moon glimmering behind a thin cloud. The night is still and the black shadows all around form strange shapes.

I quicken my pace to keep up. The dark arms of the balsam trees are heavy with snow. They reach out to touch us as we walk on.

Something stirs in the shadows beneath the branches.

"Nishiime, don't move." Nimise speaks low. "You'll scare it away."

She stops and points at a fluffy, white rabbit. But I see something bigger bounding toward us. It is moving quickly. I try to tell my sister, but the words will not come. I tug on her arm and point.

"What is it?" she asks, yet she does not look away from the rabbit.

It is too late to warn her. The huge shape is right in front of us. My sister whirls around, gasps and holds on to my arm. I suck in my breath and hold her arm. We stand motionless as we stare into the eyes of a deer.

The deer looks at us and does not move away. With strong legs, she paws at the snow before us. She waits a moment, then turns and runs gracefully toward the river.

We stare after the deer for a long time before Nimise whispers. "A white-tailed deer, nothing to be afraid of." Sister lets go of my arm.

"I know." I whisper too. "I wasn't afraid." I let go of her arm and smile. She smiles back.

We hold hands and run toward Coyote Hill. The closer we get, the more it looks like a big white bear.

When we reach the hill, Nimise says, "It's steep. Let me pull you up."

It is not that steep, but I like my big sister pulling me up. I pretend she is a team of huskies as she climbs higher, with me in tow.

"Faster. Faster." I try to call out gently, and I begin to giggle.

Nimise stops and says, "It's your turn to pull me."

"No it's not. It's my turn to be the leader, though. Follow me," I shout. I run past her as fast as I can to the top of the hill.

"Nishiime, whisper when you speak." Sister's words chase behind me.

We can see our north country for miles from Coyote Hill. The wind is strong up here. Icy fingers pull at my warm green parka. A snow cloud hides Grandmother Moon and delicate snowflakes begin to sprinkle down to us.

My sister opens her arms and reaches for the sky, trying to gather as many flakes as she can. I too reach my arms to the sky to gather my share.

She leans over and speaks. Her words are as soft and light as the snowflakes.

"The SkySpirits will come tonight."

"When?" I ask. But there is no time for an answer.

A howl breaks the silent night. Then another. The cries are long and loud. I quiver and move closer to my sister.

"What is it?" I speak so that I can barely hear my own words.

Sister's eyes are wide with excitement. "It's a coyote!" she bursts out. "He's singing to us. Listen." The coyote sings his song once again and stops.

"He's waiting for an answer," says Nimise. She cups her hands around her mouth. I do the same, and together we howl back the coyote song. Low at first, then louder. The coyote answers. So do we. A few more calls, and then all is quiet.

My sister and I look at each other and grin. Nimise's grin is as big as mine.

The wind blows stronger now and whips my scarf in circles around my head. Sister's hair falls free from her hat and swirls about her face. Her purple scarf twists and turns behind her. She leans into the wind and stretches her arms out to me. We join hands. Around and around we spin. Faster and faster. Our legs lift with the wind as we dance under the northern sky.

Dizzy, we fall down on Mother Earth's winter quilt. We lie in silence beneath the endless miles of midnight. The wind has left. It is calm again. The only sound is our breathing.

I want to ask, *When will the SkySpirits come?* But I do not speak. I like the quiet. I see the Little Dipper and follow it with my mittened hand. Nimise traces the Big Dipper. Then she says, "They'll be here soon." I wonder how she knows.

And so we wait, our faces turned to the stars. We begin to make snow angels. Our arms and legs wave at the sky. Up and down we move. Watching. Waiting. Time stands still, on top of Coyote Hill.

Suddenly, I hear my sister exclaim, "Look. They're here!"

High above us are the SkySpirits, dressed in my favorite green and Nimise's blue. We watch them sway and flicker in the four directions. Streamers of pink and purple swirl and flow across the sky. Twisting and turning, the SkySpirits join together. Around and around they spin. Faster and faster. Their shimmering parkas and scarves lift with the wind as they dance in the northern sky.

They wave down to us. And we wave back. Over and over.

I watch in silent wonder as I think of the words of our Nokomis.
Wisdom comes on silent wings.

My sister's shout breaks my tranquil thoughts.

"Nishiime, they're *SkySisters*!" Her voice echoes in the night.

"Shh," I say. "Remember, Nimise, whisper when you speak."

And we laugh out loud as we lie beneath the Northern Lights, my sister and I.